NEVER TAKE A SHARK TO THE DENTIST

NEVER TAKE A SHARK TO THE DENTIST

JUDI BARRETT AND JOHN NICKLE

SIMON AND SCHUSTER
LONDON   NEW YORK   SYDNEY

NEVER take a shark to the dentist.

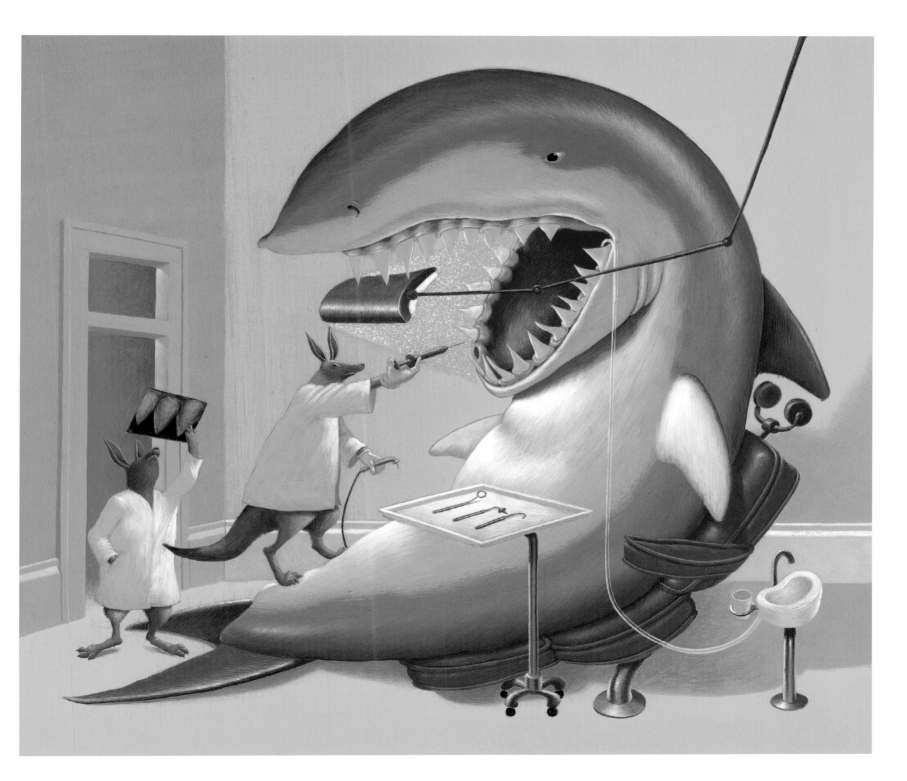

NEVER sit next to a **porcupine** on the **underground.**

NEVER

go shopping for **shoes**

with a *centipede*.

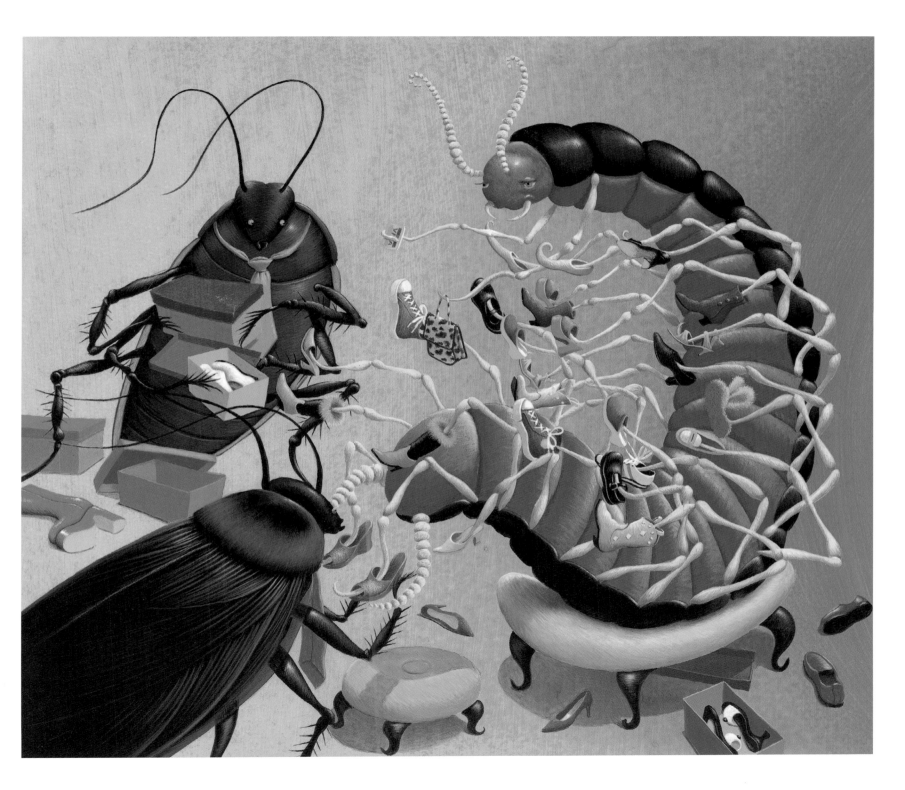

NEVER
knit a **hat**
for a moose.

NEVER
invite an _{ant}
to a **picnic.**

NEVER take a giraffe to the cinema.

NEVER
play **draughts**
with a spider.

NEVER share your lunch with a pig.

NEVER
play **skipping** with a grasshopper.

NEVER hold **hands** with a **lobster.**

NEVER take a **goat** to the **library.**

NEVER

give a *moth*

a **jumper** for

her birthday.

NEVER
go to the **bank**
with a RACCOON.

But **ALWAYS** go **shopping** with a *pelican*.

To Sasha – JB

To Brianna – JN

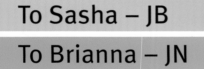

SIMON AND SCHUSTER • First published in Great Britain in 2008 by Simon and Schuster UK Ltd
Africa House, 64-78 Kingsway, London WC2B 6AH • A CBS company • Originally published in 2008
by Atheneum Books for Young Readers, an imprint of Simon & Schuster Children's Publishing
Division, New York • Text copyright © 2008 Judi Barrett • Illustrations copyright © 2008 John Nickle
The rights of Judi Barrett and John Nickle to be identified as the author and illustrator of this work
have been asserted by them in accordance with the Copyright, Designs and Patents Act, 1988
All rights reserved, including the right of reproduction in whole or in part in any form • A CIP
catalogue record for this book is available from the British Library • ISBN: 978 1 84738 320 4
Printed in Singapore • 10 9 8 7 6 5 4 3 2 1